FALLING IS EASY

FALLING IS EASY

a novella in 2 parts & 3 poems

ZELDA LEAH GATUSKIN

First Printing, 2024
ISBN: 978-0-938513-77-3
Library of Congress Control Number: 2023949070

WORLDWIND BOOKS
an imprint of
AMADOR PUBLISHERS, LLC
Albuquerque, New Mexico, USA
www.amadorbooks.com

FALLING IS EASY

MAKING THE WORST OF THINGS

Prologue

You know that old movie, *Brigadoon*? Well, I'm the Van Johnson character, the indulgent buddy who lives to tell the tale. Yes, lives—as opposed to the Gene Kelly character, who is a dead man by the end. I know, I know—it's fiction. One is supposed to believe that the mythical, magical Brigadoon takes our hero into its charm, to come awake every hundred years for a day.

A forever, if sporadic, paradise? It sounds like a place more doomed than blessed to me. I am unable to suspend my disbelief when it comes to a past and place all clean and musical like Brigadoon. The past is a din, a dust heap, a place of bondage.

Popular culture is full of male fantasies of a romantic age when women were spunky yet ultimately submissive; sexy but virtuous; had a narrowly defined role and cheerfully fulfilled it. In *Brigadoon*, those charming latter-day creatures are contrasted unflatteringly with a contemporary brand of vain, cosmopolitan, socialite harpy. Nice.

But the romantic "once upon a time" holds a place in women's imaginations as well. Oh, to be rescued, wooed, provided for and adored. To bake. Yet have an eighteen-inch waist. To do kind things for people. To have a clear path shining ahead as one assumes the role of ever-respected wife and mother.

Girlfriends, I'm here to tell you that the past is a prison. Don't go there. The protagonist of my tale didn't disappear into some magical pocket of the past. She managed to travel back in time through choice and circumstance by literally pursuing her not-uncommon fantasies. She would learn that romance with the pioneering he-man sort is way overrated, but she never could admit her error. She adopted that "Everything happens for a reason" line, and the worse things got the more fatalistic she became.

Listen to me, ladies: The next time someone you care about says, "Everything happens for a reason," insist that they see a shrink. Soon. Sure, everything happens for a reason, but it's not some Higher Power or Grand Plan reason. It's either a series of events you had no control over, or something you seriously screwed up or helped to screw up by some action of your own. Let's face it, the only time you hear "Everything happens for a reason" is when someone's life is sucking and they need "a reason" to keep going.

If only I could go back to each of those times my good friend said to me "Everything happens for a reason" and try harder to talk some sense into her. But that ship has sailed. And in spite of everything, I doubt she would do things differently if she had the chance. "Spiritual" people are proud that way.

I'm quite sure she would disapprove of me putting quotes around "spiritual," and I suspect she would not want her story to be used as a morality tale. Which means we'll come out even, she and I—we'll both have ignored the other's wishes. In any case, she can't stop me. She's gone to Brigadoon.

Lynn

Lynn was the one who always reserved the big round booth for six at the Harlequin Club for Friday night Happy Hour. You couldn't call up and ask them to save it. You had to physically show up to take the booth and start ordering—for everyone. No sitting there by your lonesome nursing a martini. If Lynn couldn't get there herself, she'd assign someone to arrive no later than four p.m., sit at the bar, scout the booth, and take possession the minute the last of the Friday liquid lunch buddies sailed off. She'd call around to the usual suspects until she found someone who could get there in time, and tell them what to order: a nice cocktail for themselves at pre-Happy Hour price, Lynn's treat; the antipasto plate for four (it took a while to put together, so didn't arrive too early); a large house pizza (ditto); and whatever they wanted right away to keep the cocktail company.

By the time Happy Hour commenced at five, three or four friends would usually have arrived to provide a respectable showing for the food, and more drink orders. By six, there might be eight or nine people squeezed in, with an extra chair or three pulled up to close the circle, creating an island of comradery in an ocean of hubbub. It was the same routine every week, and provided a rather good return on a booth for six, but the manager still wouldn't take a reservation.

If she possibly could, Lynn arrived even before four. She liked the lull. The sales force, well lubricated by that time, would tease her by lingering longer in the coveted booth. A funny kind of bond developed around this ritual.

Seeing the same faces week after week. Learning names, even. One day Lynn stopped lurking by the bar and sat down with the late lunch tipplers. She ordered coffee for them and they treated her to a drink. It became something of a tradition. She discovered that they were sales reps for office equipment.

Joel would come straight from work, which would mark the official changing of the guard. The couple might even catch a few minutes to sit alone at the big round table laden with food. They created their own private space while the tables around them filled up and the decibels increased. They were an unlikely pair, the sort that makes you look twice and make up scenarios in your head. When Joel doffed his suit jacket and tie, loosened the collar and rolled up the sleeves of his fine cotton or silk shirt—one is almost tempted to say blouse, those shirts hung so elegantly on his thin frame—he cut a graceful, bohemian figure. He wore the stubbly beard and long hair that were popular in a groomed, not-grungy style, often sporting a ponytail or man-bun.

With her short, gelled-upward hairdo, Lynn looked the tougher of the two. She liked to wear souvenir t-shirts from anywhere or any event, always a form-fitting one-size-too-small, which lent them an ironic rather than sentimental air. On Friday nights she was usually in jeans, but she had assembled an entire wardrobe around those t-shirts, from her own version of the business suit to evening wear. With perfect accessories and fabulous shoes, Lynn had a look that could not be duplicated. She was sexy to men and women, and was an equal-opportunity heartbreaker.

Having made a splash with her t-shirt techniques, Lynn was now able to live comfortably on the proceeds of her kits, how-to books and website ad revenue. She had devised ways to cut off or open up the always-too-close ribbed collar to make a lovely neckline finished with a variety of trims, usually something dainty like lace, beadwork or embroidery to contrast with the humble garment. On equal footing financially, the couple had a model modern relationship of shared but not standard domestic effort.

They had a beautiful apartment with a Lynn wing and a Joel wing, so they could indulge their own and each other's tastes entirely, and they compromised on the bedroom, living room and kitchen with a remarkable unity of opinion regarding "blandly attractive"—Joel's term. They had even been obliquely referred to in a long piece about contemporary courtship in *The Fishbowl* as "gender-busting neo-romantics," for which they endured much friendly teasing.

Lynn felt a deep contentment with Joel, especially on these Friday nights when they reigned as king and queen of the Round Table, and no one cared who was king and who was queen. In every way, Joel was exceedingly compatible, and she didn't want to break his heart. She was always relieved when he arrived, so she could shrug off the tingling allure of admiring glances to give him her full attention and bask in his.

Patty and Ellie usually arrived on the early side. Their traditional goof on the illustrious couple was to surround them in the booth to pet and squabble over whose was whose. The women made soaps and lotions at home, which were now sold exclusively on-line. They came into town just for the confab at the Harlequin, where they blew off quite a lot of steam accumulated over a week of excess togetherness.

Then there was the museum crew, who didn't get out of work until six. Clayford, Rhiannon and Mateo were the regulars, but they often brought dates or other friends from the staff. The jocks showed up late, after racket ball or handball or whatever, but before Happy Hour ended at seven.

(Where was I in this mix? Since I worked as a temp, could be any slot. In a new assignment I might be shooed out early before the office was locked up; but regular clients sometimes brought me in to help with a Friday deadline that invariably went long, so I'd miss the Round Table entirely. In that case, someone would usually call to "check in" and end up dishing me all kinds of gossip. If I missed a Friday gathering, you can be sure that by Monday I knew more about what was going on with everyone than anyone who'd been there.)

On the nights when the Round Table sported the full complement, Lynn would look around at her friends, then beyond to the club generally, and feel flushed with pride (and maybe a few *mojitos*) at how *evolved* we were. In her own lifetime, in her own life, she had seen the gender gap not only close but overlap. Sexuality, identity, roles, personality—it was all mix-and-match now. Lynn remembered the feminine stereotype she'd rebelled against not so many years before, and was thrilled at her generation's collective rejection of the old gender templates. Now everyone could be themselves. Creative, authentic, open and equal.

Except that Lynn was ever our fearless leader.

The liquid lunch crew dealt with Lynn's voluptuous

androgyny by treating her like one of the guys. She had razzed them about not having any women on their team, and they responded by trying to recruit her, regaling her with the scintillating details of high-speed copiers, and assuring her that female colleagues did exist, just not any who were into the Friday "week-cap." Lynn could certainly believe that part. The men had the air of the last century about them. Unfashionable but not cheap suits, slightly rumpled, the ties loosened and endlessly varied.

Lynn imagined each man selecting the day's tie from a rack overflowing with a decade's worth of gifts. All had children. Not all currently married. Not all young or all old. But Lynn observed that the suit, tie, haircut and shave made them all identical Mr. Cleavers, ageless. They were holdouts in a doomed profession. Everything was done on-line now. Who actually shlepped from place to place with sample kits anymore?

Lynn imagined sitcom lives for the men. And when the husbands slugged down a coffee or a coke and headed out, hurrying now, suddenly aware of time, she envied their fictitious wives. Someone was home cooking dinner or dolling herself up for a night out. In that moment when she waited for Joel and the others to arrive, alone at the Round Table—a queen without subjects—yes, Lynn sometimes envied those wives, the ones she imagined, the way she imagined them: simple, provided for, pretty in a formulaic way. Being bisexual was complicated. Everything times two, right? Being conventionally identified was more like filling a mold. You fill your spot and he fills his, and then the two of you fit together and make a unit, something strong. You don't have to be everything, you just have to be half. It would be easier, right?

These thoughts—like residual dust of previous generations, Lynn told herself—would disperse with the appearance of Joel. He was beautiful in his suit and out of it. She wasn't simple and neither was he. They complemented and challenged each other. They also made a unit, a strong one with more interlocking parts—two integrated wholes combining, not two half-beings.

The sales force, should any linger so long, observed the couple's attraction and devotion as they greeted each other. It was a head-scratcher. Joel looked gay to them. Lynn too, but she had a hot body. Joel's wasn't bad either, when he rolled up those sleeves—

Lynn and Joel. Yep, a head-scratcher and a crotch-tingler. Sober up, scamper out. No one had the balls to make a pass at Lynn. One or two may have considered making a pass at the couple, but never spoke of it or acted on it. Lynn was safe with the sales force. Joel found it amusing. Until the day he was late, and they'd brought a new recruit along.

"Everything happens for a reason," Lynn said later.

The attraction between Lynn and Rob was immediate, intense, indecent and short lived. It lasted exactly until the Friday that Rob, at Lynn's insistence, stuck around for Happy Hour. He moved over to the bar to observe her crowd and decide if he wanted to be introduced. The previous two Fridays, the combustible chemistry between Lynn and Rob had been palpable to the point of unsettling the liquid lunch crew. The gentlemen had cut short their stay at the round table and hustled Rob out to insure there would be no overlap with any of Lynn's set, especially Joel. But, as it happened, when Rob finally saw Joel in the flesh, and saw Lynn with Joel, his ardor was so quickly and thoroughly cooled that his coworkers regretted their precautions. On that third Friday, Rob sat at the bar for about half an hour carefully avoiding Lynn's furtive glances, then slipped out when she wasn't looking. It was the last time they ever saw each other. Rob bowed out of the Friday lunches, and the sales force was greatly relieved.

But the flirtation had incited Lynn's need for conquest. The couple's bi style hadn't turned Rob on, she reported, it had repelled him. This was over coffee the following week: Lynn speculating that Rob had latent homosexual tendencies and was disturbed to find himself attracted to Joel. Me suggesting that Rob simply realized Lynn was unavailable.

I hadn't been making it to the Round Table for a few months, due to a long-term assignment across town. Lynn and I had gotten into the habit of meeting at one of the places near my work, and I had started to prefer these one-on-ones to being at the actual event. This way, Lynn could regale me not only with all of the gossip exchanged, but with all of the gossip generated in the Friday evening festivities. There was another advantage, in that I was certain not to be one of the stars or supporting actors in any of the episodes, although I had no doubt that any juicy tidbits Lynn could glean about my personal life would be a feature of next Friday's gathering. Still, it would have been nice to get a gander at Rob.

Lynn claimed that, other than being aware these were the guys who sometimes tied up the table long into the afternoon, our friends were oblivious to the late lunch crew, "the LLs." I didn't doubt it, since I'd learned more about the salesmen from Lynn's reports than I'd ever observed when I attended the Round Table. But there had been silence on that front for several weeks, up until this particular coffee date when the Rob saga spilled forth. Suddenly I was getting a lengthy monologue about how hot the guy was, and how his attention turned Lynn on, and her feeling of teetering on the edge—like the feeling of reaching the top of a long climb in a roller-coaster, and the intense thrill that was like fear—or was it the other way around?

She wound herself up to that moment when Rob was at the far side of the bar looking over towards the Round Table, able to see everyone who came over, and how the others jumped up to greet each new arrival. She had wanted Rob to see her greet Joel, and to accept that she was in a committed relationship; to see her friends, and accept that Rob and she came from different planets and had no business pursuing each other.

So Lynn had rationalized. But in her disappointment at Rob's disappearance from the scene, she had to admit to herself that she'd actually hoped that seeing the affection between herself and Joel would stimulate Rob all the more. Lynn wanted to tease Rob for the sheer pleasure of it. And she told me that the idea of doing so actually made her "even hotter for Joel."

When Lynn concluded with, "Everything happens for a reason," I thought she meant that, in spite of her intentions, Rob had been put off by seeing the happy couple and was spurred to get out of the picture pronto. I did *not* think it meant that the reason the fantasy affair had happened was to make Lynn realize that she needed more macho lust in her life.

The change that came over Lynn following the Rob obsession appeared to be aimed at strengthening her relationship with Joel by adding more sexual excitement. She kept at her t-shirt design business, which Joel admired, but gave up the style for herself. She started wearing more elegant, feminine, business wear—silks and linens, tailored skirts and suits. She and Joel "matched better." He cut his hair, she grew hers. They made an even more attractive couple. She explained that she and Joel had decided to change things up—well, she had suggested and he agreed. It wasn't about him, or her, they'd just gotten too comfortable. If their relationship was really "fluid" they should be able to "play" with their "gender affect"—it would re-ignite their passion. But Lynn's energies were probably, perhaps unknowingly, already aimed away from Joel. It wasn't long before her new look attracted the sort of attention she desired.

Something interesting happened with Lynn's business at this same time: The more traditionally and tastefully Lynn herself dressed, the better the clientele for her funky artisan t-shirts. Doors literally opened for her. She began arranging home shopping events in which well-connected women invited well-off women friends to catered affairs at their homes. When Lynn came in dressed very much like the suave ladies themselves, they immediately trusted her. She easily coaxed them into her playful creations, and coached them on how to work these unique garments into their wardrobes, so that they were utterly charmed by what they saw in the mirror. Funny how Lynn's attempts to advertise the tees on her own body had never worked with the upper-echelon crowd. They'd had no desire to look like Lynn until she began to look like them.

After one of our coffee dates, at which Lynn regaled me in super self-congratulatory detail about this latest business venture, I wondered if her whole upcycled t-shirt idea hadn't become rather too ironic. She had apparently spent much of her profits on a new wardrobe for herself that was about as far from the humble t-shirt as a body could get. I was sufficiently rankled to arrange a half-day off so I could join the Friday Round Table and see what the rest of the crew thought of the new Lynn.

It had been a while since any of them had called me. They knew that Lynn and I met fairly often, as she always passed along my regards and news, so maybe they didn't feel the need to check in. But I suspected something more. Clarissa, who worked at the museum, seemed uneasy the last time we'd spoken. She'd missed a few Fridays and was calling to feel me out about something that she managed never to say in words. Lots of *uhms* and *anyways* and *whatevers*. Allusions to the way Lynn ordered for everyone, paid for everything, made her seem more condescending than generous. And clothes came up more than once, how differently Lynn was dressed. Well, I'd already noticed both changes for myself. I asked about Joel. "Sweet," Clarissa said. "He's just so sweet." I had a feeling she was sweet on him herself (weren't we all?) but, in retrospect, I think it was pity. Those who had lately seen Lynn and Joel together could guess what was coming.

It was in this unsettled atmosphere of unspoken knowledge that I found my friends when I joined them at the Round Table. I sensed a bit of suspicion when they greeted me, despite their sincere warmth, as though I might be a spy or appointee of her highness Lynn. Our lady had yet to arrive, and had uncharacteristically failed to contact anyone about saving the table. It was pure luck that Patty and Ellen had arrived soon enough to claim it from "the Dads" (that's what they called Lynn's "LLs"), who had also been concerned about Lynn's absence. I had no clue as to what had become of her either. We settled in, feeling good in each other's company, but uneasy also, not knowing who knew what or noticed what or suspected what. Food and drink and formulaic talk kept our mouths occupied while our minds raced.

Lynn swept in at last, breathless and seeming to sprout shopping bags from more limbs than she possessed. "Sorry, sorry, sorry, everyone!" she exclaimed, and then, seeing me, "Oh, Nancy, you're here! Perfect! I have the most incredible news! I'm going to Paris!"

Much scooting around the booth and chair-scraping and making room for packages around our feet, all of us looking from her to the restaurant entrance to her to each other. Finally, someone, maybe it was even me, asked about Joel.

"Oh, he's not coming." Her manner could not have been more breezy.

"To Happy Hour or to Paris?"

That question was definitely posed by me. I surprised myself with the harsh tone in which it came out, and I regretted it. But the others were looking at me with relief, like I had spoken something that had been quietly brewing among them.

"Neither," Lynn answered just as sharply. Then, seeing the alarm on our faces, she sighed and sank back against the padded back of the booth. Casting aside affectation, the sincere, uncompromising Lynn we loved returned just long enough to tell us, "The problem with living with someone is that when things get rocky you're not sure whether you need to break up or get married. And the problem specifically with me and Joel is, I would actually get married, but he wants to break up."

We were unanimously speechless.

"So, I'm going to Paris to immerse myself in the world of fashion. I have a sponsor and a place to stay. Oh, and I have a new name, *mes amis*, I've decided to go by Gwen instead of Lynn. You'll have plenty of time to get used to it. I'll write you every day and sign off as Gwen, and we'll all be used to it when I'm back in six weeks."

At this point, we were still not saying anything, because we were slugging our drinks. Someone, Mateo maybe, managed to blurt out, "But why?"

"Because I'm working my way up to the full Gwendolynn. So much more distinctive than Lynn, especially for a designer. I'll go from Lynn to Gwen informally, and then use Gwendolynn for my label."

The restaurant was super noisy by this time, but folks at nearby tables, some of them also regulars, could not help but notice the icy silence that suddenly descended over the Round Table. It spread, slowing and muffling nearby conversations as it radiated outward from our arctic circle. Lynn was rifling through her vast purse-briefcase in search of samples of the new Gwendolynn font treatment, oblivious to the ice age her news bomb was causing. (Not long after this "the full Gwendolyn" would enter our private lexicon, loosely translating to "snow job.")

Ray, bless his heart, brought us back to our senses and good humor. "I see," he said. "So you're looking for a bridge from Lynn to Gwendolynn. How about you just call yourself Doh!" Everyone cracked up, except you know who.

Gwen

At least she didn't make a secret of the fact that she was remaking herself. And she did write often, if not every day, a group email to the Round Table—actually sent to just one of us every Thursday, for the purpose of being read aloud at Happy Hour. Insubordinate as we were, whoever received the message would forward it to everyone else. It was also this person's job to copy and paste our responses into a reply, to be sent after the convening of the Round Table, so that attendance could be reported. And so we kept up the facade that all of *us* and our relationships were unchanged, despite Lynn's transformation to Gwen, then Gwen's departure to France, and the absence of dear Joel altogether. We kept up appearances by calling her every so often whenever any of us were together anywhere, especially if it meant we would be ringing her in the middle of the night.

I wonder when we might have learned about David, had we not taken such pleasure in disturbing Gwen's *bon nuits* in the City of Love. She was obviously shacking up with someone or he with her. She had first traveled in the company of two of her new "T-Time" patrons, who brought her along for a long weekend at their friend's condo in Troyes. Their hostess was a fashion industry executive who had been persuaded to take up Gwen's cause. The four women proceeded to Paris and Gwen was introduced to everyone (if I may summarize). While the other three ladies had plans for a reunion jaunt to the Riviera, Gwen intended to stay on in Paris to study or teach or something—a talk here, a collaboration there, an interview, a fact-finding market-testing thingy. Honestly, it wasn't so murky. She spared us no details, but we couldn't take in any of them. She had gone very far away. Then she came home with David, the debonair ex-husband (as it turned out) of the *fashionista* with the flat.

Gwen was quick to assure us that she hadn't broken up the marriage. The couple had been divorced for years, but remained friends. In any case, it was impossible to avoid each other in Paris, where shared business concerns and must-attend cultural events often caused their paths to cross. *"Tres enlightement, n'cest pas?"*

Gwen's French was atrocious. Her taste was anything but. Certainly nothing about David cast suspicion on her taste in men. He was a little older, a lot taller, hardly any suaver, but overall noticeably more masculine than Joel. Equally nice. Interesting enough—that is, far less interesting than Gwen, just as she liked it. And, exactly in proportion to his extra manliness quotient, that much more fawning and seductive in his attention to "Gwen" than Joel had been to "Lynn."

It wasn't hard to like David, however he compared to Joel, but Gwen herself took some getting used to. Did we remember her so poorly that her physical presence was a shock to us? Looking around the table I could read the same confusion in my friends' expressions as plagued me. We were all trying to draw up a correct picture in our minds of the dark-haired, shapely, average-height Lynn to compare to the statuesque, blond Gwen clinging to David's arm. He, as a stranger, made more sense to us than our old friend.

"Nice shoes," Patty said, wanting to get a look at exactly how high those heels were.

Gwen obliged by pushing her chair back and standing to pose. (I think that pair of shoes cost more than my car.) I was belatedly impressed by her gracefulness, because it could not have been easy to glide along on those spikes. Perhaps the mere effort of walking explained the muscular curve of her calf, but the overall smooth, tight tone of Gwen's golden limbs suggested masseuses and trainers, swimming and sunning.

"Your hair looks cool," Ellie pitched in.

What could we do but *ooh* and *ahh* over her?

Well, Ray, at least, decided to take the measure of the man. David had jumped up when Gwen stood to show off her shoes. Such a gentleman. He would not sit as long as she was standing, so he hovered over her while she flipped her hair around and talked about the marvelous

French salons.

"Doh!" Ray popped up from deep inside the round booth, and everyone had to get up and suck in their lower halves while he worked his way around, with much poking and giggling, to where David and Gwen stood at the open end of the booth. If you hadn't been there on that earlier Friday that seemed so long ago but was only eight weeks past, you would've just thought he was grunting with the exertion. Gwen gave him a look that said *no fair* but Ray didn't see it. He was right in David's face, pushing past him while he gave some lame excuse about something he had forgotten. A brief but unmistakable "moment of dude," as Clayford called it later (Ray himself called it "sniffing butts"), at the end of which Ray broke free, grabbed Gwen in a bear hug that lifted her off those fiendish shoes, dropped her back into her seat, and spun around with his hand outstretched to David.

"Good to meet ya, dude. Catch ya later."

And he was off. David sat, dazed, and rubbed his right hand. The rest of us reached for our drinks.

I could not wait to talk to Ray.

"He's a lightweight, Nance. I could take him, for sure."

"Seriously? Your whole assessment of a man is based

on which of you could beat up the other?"

"Absolutely."

"And I thought you were one of the enlightened ones."

"No way, Princess. A man's gotta do what a man's gotta do."

Let me say here that this is the kind of conversation I tended to have with Ray. It was during our flirtation period, but neither of us would admit we were serious. We bantered a lot about guy-stuff and girl-stuff, so as to keep in the forefront that we were one of each, I suppose, and the idea that we might someday fit together.

"And what exactly does a man gotta do?" I inquired.

"Give his girl-buddy's new dude the old sniff test."

"And?" Really, I was curious. I had not gotten any read at all on David in the hour we had spent drinking and eating together, except that he was nice and hadn't seemed to have altered Gwen any more than she had altered herself, which was mostly external. We had all settled in and had a nice time. Could Ray really have learned more just by acting like a jerk for a couple of minutes?

"He's not a bully. He's not a snob. He's a dude. With money. And he likes chicks. Why do you suppose he divorced the first wife, if she even was the first?"

"I don't know, and how could you?"

"He had his eyes all over that place. You didn't catch him giving you the once-over?"

"Well, yeah, maybe." I had been vain enough to think it was just me, if not for my looks, then because I was first among Gwen's loyal friends.

"Yeah, well. I'm afraid he's going to drop our Gwen-Doh-Lynn as quickly as he scooped her up. Not to worry, though. She's not that into him."

"Ray, how can you possibly—"

"I just know, Nance. I just know."

I had never liked anyone calling me Nance before, but when Ray did... Well, that's how love is, I guess. I kept him on the phone a little longer just to hear him say it again.

Ray was right. He knew Lynn better than Lynn knew herself. Or should I say, he knew Gwen better than Lynn knew her. Gwen was looking for passion, but she hadn't counted on how fast that kind of fire can burn out. And she sure as hell wasn't into sharing. She thought that would be clear to David when she married him.

The wedding took place in Las Vegas, and some of us erstwhile loyal subjects made the trip. They made a stunning pair, Gwen and David, every bit as gorgeous as Lynn and Joel, but entirely different. It wasn't difficult to call her Gwen after that. And it was easier to believe that she had wanted to marry Joel, but he had refused. Whether by wisdom or prescience, he could read the writing on the wall. Lynn had felt her own attachment weakening and thought she could literally tie herself to him and secure their future together. Joel thought (he told me this himself) he could cut her loose to have her flings and test her limits, and then maybe she would come back, and maybe they would see that the separation had been painful but necessary, and maybe they could start again. Maybe.

Lynn had never been a *maybe* kind of person, and her least favorite *maybe* was *maybe I'll change my mind*. She changed her mind as much as the rest of us do, or more so, but this never came in the form of regret. To insure there would be no remorse or reverting to a previous position, she would leave wreckage in her wake. Once she had decided it was time to move on, she systematically dismantled everything. She was capable of introspection, and not a dummy about pinpointing what specific aspects of her life were unsatisfactory, but her approach was slash and burn—the problem element could not be improved unless everything was renovated. Maybe Lynn could have had a fling with David, gone globe-trotting, even become a mega-star on the fashion scene, and still gone back to Joel. But Lynn was erased, and Gwen was never going have a life with Joel or he with her.

Correction, because I'm analyzing this in retrospect, and I haven't got that quite right: Lynn had changed her appearance and her name, but she was not altogether erased. The Gwen-and-David period was only the beginning of that process. A lot of Lynn lingered, like the part that had wanted to marry Joel so as not be at the mercy of her crushes—as though vows would protect her and monogamous love would win out over random lusts. She was willing to give up the vanity of flirtation for a single sexy, solicitous partner. That is, she was willing to try, and when Joel wouldn't try it out with her, she— Gwen—tried David. David might have felt the same way. He really was a nice guy. All his wives agreed.

(Yeah, Ray had David pegged. Still, we had an excellent time at the wedding.)

When Gwen wouldn't put up with David's dalliances, he divorced her as good-naturedly as he'd married her. They had been together two years. She took the failed marriage in stride, never looked back. The two years had been eventful—quite useful, really. She had traveled the world, and made the most of her travels by seeking out important sites both famous and obscure, and applying herself to the study of each region's history and culture.

She kept a journal. She took lessons in watercolor painting. She designed more clothing, not based on the t-shirt. And, in secret, she began to write poetry.

"Why in secret?" I wondered, when she finally confessed this sin to me.

"Because I felt like everything in my life had been right on the surface since—forever, I guess. I might be changeable, but whatever I am, it's all out there. Obviously I like the attention, like being praised. I even kind of like being trashed. You know, just giving the world a jolt."

That sounded like the old Lynn, and I smiled and said so, which clearly bugged her. She shook her head like I didn't get it, and I didn't.

"Sorry, what were you saying about the poetry?"

"It was mine. My secret. I have an inner life too, you know."

I was beginning to feel like I'd been a crappy friend. But then she laid that "Everything happens for a reason" line on me, and a bunch of red lights and warning bells went off. So, what does a friend do at that point?

I bit my tongue and put my arm around her. We were the only two people occupying the booth at the Harlequin Club, and not expecting anyone else. The place was filling up, but the manager was leaving us alone. I noticed him pat his small vest pocket from time to time; no doubt it held a big bill he didn't want to forget about. The instant our glasses were empty, a young server appeared out of nowhere and adeptly poured our champagne. The chef himself or his sous-chef visited us periodically with bites from the kitchen. Yes, Gwen had returned from her marriage and divorce a wealthy woman.

(I was surprised that David could support so many ex-wives. In fact, he couldn't. The Gwendolynn line had made a bit of a splash in Europe, and two of David's exes went in together to buy the label. Gwen had lost her interest in fashion by that time. She thought this outcome was hilarious, and called the transaction "hand-me-down alimony." In retrospect, again, I can only see the sale of her business as another instance of my friend burning her bridges.)

"I'm going to miss you. You just got back." She was moving to Oregon for a post-grad program in Creative Writing at a small, prestigious college. Now the poetry secret was out, and I was proud of her.

"I'm proud of you."

"Thank you, Nancy. Let's get drunk."

"Let's call the old gang to come join us. You can afford another bottle or two."

"Oh, I don't know."

"C'mon. A welcome-home and a send-off all at once. From your loyal swains." We were already rather tipsy, and I was feeling magnanimous with her money. "C'mon, Lynn—no—doh!—Gwen!"

She humored me while I texted everyone, and I could tell she was pleased that they all managed to show up on this non-Friday, and reassured by the sincere pleasure they expressed in seeing her. But we of the Round Table were already two identities removed from the new woman who was heading west to become a poet. Even at the time I could sense this. The others could too, I think.

When the time came to part, there were no promises of correspondence or instructions for future Round Table assemblies. We had the impression we were being dismissed. There was a decided feeling of finality.

Gwendolynn

As befitting a poet, she kept the long form of her name. Surprisingly, she did keep in touch with her old gang, usually writing to me but sometimes others, and always in a friendly, confidential tone addressed to all. She even signed off *Lynn,* although she assured us that in her new milieu she strictly enforced the use of Gwendolynn, no nicknames allowed. She said she liked goofing on her mostly younger classmates and mostly older professors, whom she found surprisingly similar in their excess of politeness, practiced sensitivity and righteous objectivity. We had no cause to doubt her—her digital signature included her preferred pronouns (she/her) and title (Ms.) above a brilliantly funny Ven Diagram of Appropriate Greeting Behavior from air kisses to bear hugs.

We sensed Lynn's discomfort behind all this bravado. The environment was entirely strange to her—more unsettling than her many adventures in foreign countries, where the language of money was always understood and the speaker of that language always accommodated. Our friend was finding the language and society of academia harder to crack. We sympathized and cheered her on; and when the correspondence dwindled away, we figured she had triumphed over adversity and attracted another crew of loyal subjects to take our place.

There were no hard feelings or recriminations on our part. The Round Table continued to meet, monthly now instead of weekly. Joel returned. After reconnecting, he brought a boyfriend to the next gathering. You can imagine our surprise. The charming young man was quickly welcomed into the fold. The funny thing is, next to him Joel looked almost macho, although he had changed his look very little. I don't think any of us ever shared this juicy news with Lynn, although we never agreed not to, or even discussed it outright. My own feeling was that this was exactly the sort of turn-around that Lynn would find a turn-on, and I did not want her sweeping back into Joel's life out of some perverse curiosity or need to reconquer. In any case, she never once asked directly about Joel, so I had no reason to volunteer anything.

Following a lull in correspondence through the winter and early-spring months of Lynn's first year in her MFA program, we were gratified to receive a fat packet of actual print material in evidence of her effort. There was a hefty literary magazine on glossy paper representing the finest of the Creative Writing majors' work, within which were buried two poems by Gwendolynn. There were also some back issues of a local arts-entertainment rag with her witty film reviews, and a thin chapbook of prose essays about her world travels. This was by far the best of the work, but it seemed to me the pieces had been taken from her journals almost verbatim—I recognized some of the passages from our earlier correspondence.

As for the poetry, well, after these treasures were duly circulated, we didn't discuss it. I tried to get Rhiannon to explain it to me, because I considered her the most literary of our group. She cringed and said, "Maybe they call that sort of thing erotica now. There is a mathematical precision to it. I mean, it shows craft, but, yuk. Poetry is supposed to lift its subject, however mundane, out of the everyday sphere—but those are more like a trip to the gynecologist."

"You almost wish they were more raunchy." What I meant was, they didn't even sound like Lynn, Gwen, whoever. But maybe Gwendolynn had even made over her vagina, so as to accommodate a larger vocabulary.

Rhiannon was unwilling to talk more about the poetry or its author, but she made a short speech that I have given quite a lot of thought to in the time since. She said: "Universities are full of creeps with patches on their elbows who are eager to help young women *achieve their potential.* No matter what department they are attached to, they will at some point admonish said female student that she doesn't *want it enough* and hasn't *sufficient fire inside* to *make it* and might possibly just be a little *frigid*—you know, in the *artistic* sense—and ought to be calling upon her *sexual energy* to launch her to *new heights* of creative expression."

I responded with something like, "I'm sure Lynn can hold her own against any profs who are coming on to her."

Rhiannon wasn't buying it: "Sure, an honest-to-god pass, but I could see someone getting his rocks off by wheedling that shit erotica out of his female students. Who knows, maybe the guys too."

"Huh."

"Academia is a cesspool of sexism, Nancy."

"I don't know. When I was—"

"Trust me."

So we left it there.

Gwendolynn stayed on the West Coast through summer break, and in the fall she was back to work and back to writing to us now and then. A certain poetry professor was mentioned frequently and with growing familiarity. He was the previous year's prof, and she called him Philip. Meanwhile, under the tutelage of a different instructor (a woman, I should add), her poetry was improving. By spring semester, she was dropping hints about a romantic relationship with Philip, a widower with two children. By graduation they were engaged.

None of us went to the wedding. Who knows, maybe it brought this marriage better luck. By every indication, Gwendolynn and Philip had a fabulous life together for more than ten years. They came out to the east coast now and then, so acquaintances were made.

He was an older man, nice looking, not condescending that I could tell, and not smarmy. But he sure had our Lynn—his Gwendolynn—in his thrall. She positively worshipped him, and he absolutely loved that about her and rewarded her for it. I visited them once and saw the beautiful life they had made together. I was especially impressed with the son and daughter, teenagers by then, whom Lynn had won over with determined effort and whom she truly loved, and who loved her in return.

So, why should I be the least bit snarky about their good fortune? Had Rhiannon not made those bitter comments, would I have felt the same, either at the beginning or the end?

For it did end, tragically, with Philip dying of cancer after a prolonged decline and several desperate, debilitating rounds of treatment. Gwendolynn—the name suits her in this role—was heroic throughout. Her collapse and devastation after her husband's death must be the source of my personal disillusionment with the Philip affair. He took everything she had and left her with nothing. Oh sure, she was well set financially. But she was a wife, now a widow, and absent the husband she was diminished.

I'm convinced that not all marriages are like that. That in a marriage of equals, the two individuals stay individuals and raise each other into better, stronger people. When one partner dies there is grief beyond measure, but not loss of self.

No, none of us went to the wedding. But some of us went to the funeral. We wanted to bring Gwendolynn home with us. She said maybe she would come after the youngest was out of college. Only another semester if all went well. Well, it did go well for the kids, but not so much for their step-mom.

At loose ends without Philip or the kids to care for, Gwendolynn decided to return to some of her earlier interests. She could start by poking around the internet.

She would check out the latest fashion trends, explore some literary and art history sites, brush up on her French—it was all at her fingertips. Day after day she settled at the kitchen table with her coffee and her tablet, her browser awaiting her command.

Then she would stare blankly at the screen while her coffee got cold, unable even to muster up a search term. When the screen eventually blipped into power-save mode, she would go lie down in the ground-floor guest room.

This went on for quite a while. Over time, though, while Gwendolynn stared at the ceiling or the darkened screen, her vague thoughts began to coalesce. She contemplated how easy it had been to surrender to love and to lose herself in the needs of others. The demise of her previous relationships had not left her so vulnerable as this. With Joel, then David, her own pursuits had carried her through—the t-shirts, then more serious fashion design, then poetry. But once married to the poetry professor, she'd stepped back from her own writing to support his. No point competing. Her step-children had tapped her design talents for bedroom decor, school projects, prom-wear—there'd been no shortage of outlets for her artistic nature. She'd never felt short-changed. But now she found she had very little to show for that creative outpouring.

More time passed, and one morning Gwendolynn got dressed. The internet had proved to be a barrier, not a portal. She would go to the University library with the notes she had kept from her Gender Studies courses and work her way forward to the current wave of feminist thinking. She had toyed with the idea of picking up her poetry again, but then quickly dispensed with it. Why feminism and not poetry? The question practically answered itself. Poetry had been Philip's purview.

Was the problem that she'd felt inferior to him in that field—or that she knew she didn't dare exceed him? She had suppressed her talent for fear of... What? His jealousy? Worse. His denial. As the Authority on the Craft, what if Philip coached and critiqued Gwendolynn's poems to death, hindered her, undermined her? Deep down, she must have felt him capable of doing so. It hurt to acknowledge it. Thinking about Philip and poetry hurt in general. The idea of going to the University library, of all places, to research feminist thought lost all appeal.

But she had found her Gender Studies notes, and from them she made a list of search terms. Gwendolynn went back to the computer with purpose. She had time on her hands. She read a ton of stuff, and she wrote to me often during this period. I was (am) still a working stiff, so I couldn't keep up with the volume of literature she consumed, but I egged her on. She was on to something, and I hoped she would pursue it: Among all the classic novels, and all the recent lauded ones, Gwen was looking for role models. Had anyone ever envisioned, in fiction, a woman or a man, or a male-female relationship, that was neither weighed down by traditional gender roles nor self-consciously trying to overcome them?

"All we do is push off against that old wall that divides us into he-roles and she-roles," Gwen wrote to me. "How is a woman to find, to even imagine, an identity that is truly authentic, that comes from within, that is not a reaction to what has always been?"

I didn't have an answer to that. Still don't. Ray and I just rock and roll along like I figure every other couple in history ever did, ever will. Two people who are making a life together are either making it up as they go along, or making the best of the templates provided. Maybe alternating between the two. And from what I've observed, identity crises and power struggles are no strangers to couples of the same gender.

I suggested that Gwen might write her own book,

create that new archetype of womanhood. But look who's doing the writing. Gwen went deep, but she went backward.

Wendy

Gwendolynn picked Wendy for her screen name. (Here I sigh very, very deeply.)

Wendy's studies were segueing from feminism in general to widowhood, since that's where she was at. She wanted to find out what other people had to say about their sense of identity when they found themselves in this sad state. Her initial searches yielded long lists of social/dating sites for widows and widowers. Apparently her peers were not plumbing the depths of their souls for that core authentic wholeness that must be explored, now they were alone. They were looking for another puzzle piece to fit into the empty place. Sometimes literally a good screw.

Come to think of it, that's where Philip had been at too, she realized. Funny how she never thought of him so much as a widower, but as a single father. His first wife had died of cancer not so long before Gwendolynn showed up in his poetry class. True, by the time he finally asked her out Philip had been a widower for several years, but he'd been pursuing her one way or another for much of that time. It hadn't been difficult. Gwen intentionally put herself within reach by joining the staff of the literary journal for which he was faculty advisor.

What had Philip felt and done immediately following his first wife's death? He and Gwen never spoke of it, even when his own health was following the same trajectory. Philip was older, of course, his cancer of a different variety but equally virulent. He mainly talked about the children, how unfair for them to lose both parents, and how fortunate they were to have Gwen. At any rate, once widowed herself, Gwen was not craving a replacement puzzle piece or piece of ass any time soon. Philip and she had joined their lives together perfectly in a partnership that could never be duplicated.

As for sex, her husband's physical deterioration and her intimate duties as his caretaker haunted Gwen. She no longer hungered for a male body, or any body. A gray and withered ghost layered itself upon any hearty specimen that caught her eye, causing her to feel simultaneously disgusted and disloyal. A turn-off, to say the least. Her own body felt like a burden that her brain was dragging around without enthusiasm. It felt like a victory to simply bathe, dress and eat. She forced herself to handle the business of death, then children and college, while she kept her devices humming along with their steady stream of blogs, news services and search results.

More time passed. One day, she not only got dressed, she made herself go out for a walk. She hadn't been able to make herself sleep.

Gwen had been going everywhere in her car, unwilling to meet and speak with neighbors. It was almost agoraphobic, the way she felt panicky outdoors, especially near home. As though she didn't belong there without Philip. As though she was untethered, and might float off in search of an unreachable past, or unimaginable future, not to be seen again. (This, in a way, came true.) Even her house was too big. Only the small circuit between kitchen, study and guest room felt safe—everywhere else, she was an intruder caught in the open, caught in the floodlights, soon to be expelled. Her car had always been just hers, so she was comfortable driving places, places that were familiar to her but where she was unremarkable—those big, impersonal stores or a public park or shopping mall.

"I must be someplace I recognize where no one recognizes me," is how she had described her condition to me in a letter. Anywhere else could spark a panic attack.

As the initial depression passed, instead of only

wanting to sleep, Gwen found that she couldn't sleep at all. She knew she must get some exercise. She knew she had to get out. Not just outside, but *out* out. Out of the house she had lived in with Philip and his children. Out of the posh suburbs she would have despised in an earlier incarnation, and in which she felt exceedingly out of place as a widowed empty-nester. She would start by going outdoors very early and taking a brisk walk. She could enjoy the sunrise, exercise in solitude, and plan her next move.

But when she went for her solitary walk at dawn, Gwen found herself waving or nodding a greeting to one woman after another. She supposed they were all wives, they were out so very early. They might be escaping husbands, grabbing some personal time. Or they were missing husbands, unable to sleep, like her. Maybe they were staying in shape for husbands. That was a nice possibility to think about. The women did not intrude on Gwen, though some of them stopped briefly to talk to each other.

"Women of the Morning." Gwen thought she would try to write a poem when she got back to the house. She thought of it as "the house" now, not home. She needed to find a new home. She needed to find herself. "Women of

43

the Morning." It thrummed in her head. The walk was stirring her imagination. The morning in all its well-tended suburban glory was like a scene from a movie. The walk was therapeutic. She would get more exercise.

And yet… Gwen did not want to become a woman of the morning. She did not find it comforting to be one of many; she did not want their companionship. And the joys of nature, once the sun was high, were revealed as landscapes sculpted by humans for humans. Winding along the gardens and lawns whetted Gwen's appetite for "real" nature. Observing the other women walkers revived her questions about her own "real nature." By the time she got back to her desk other ideas had overlaid the incipient poem. Ideas that required syntax, explicitness, reasoning. She started a blog, "Wendy" did, expressing her desire to get out of society, to escape stereotypes. To be spontaneous. Authentic. Unshackled.

And that is how Bluebeard found her and lured her into his trap.

"Everything happens for a reason," Wendy wrote at the close of her final letter from Philip's suburban paradise. She was moving to the Louisiana bayou with her new beau, to rough it on an off-the-grid plot of land that would surely prove its worth once the new scenic byway went through.

I won't sully the page by typing this dreadful man's name. He was quite simply a Bluebeard through and through. Like the fairy tale heroine, our Wendy was not his first victim-wife. She was too proud to have her father and brothers come save her (they surely would have, but she had always spurned their interference). No, not too proud. Too ashamed. Wendy only hinted at the nature of her abasement, then her letters stopped entirely.

Ray and I were working on a plan to track down Lynn/Gwendolynn/Wendy when I received a *second* wedding announcement, of all things. The brief notice was clipped out of a local weekly and folded inside a note: "I have been rescued. No need to worry. Give my love to everyone. W."

I recognized my old friend in the grainy photo. Gaunt, aged, still beautiful. The tremulous expression was one I had never seen before, slightly scared but hopeful. Despite her years, this woman really looked like a new bride—one from a previous century, when men were men and women were timid. Her new husband looked rugged, to say the least. I couldn't help but envision a literal rescue removed from modern times by millennia, not centuries.

Not a knight in shining armor clashing sword and shield, but a male more like the caveman meme of old—one fur-clad Neanderthal bopping another on the head with a club, then dragging the swooning female away by the hair. The note and wedding notice cemented my sense of Lynn having de-evolved from her enlightened, bi identity. She'd traveled back in time through liberated sex goddess, revered wife, abused domestic, all the way to basic biological partner, "as nature intended."

It had been Wendy's desire to get back to nature, right? And so she did. Now she would be a She-woman coupled with a He-man eking out an existence in the boonies. Or in Brigadoon. And meanwhile the rest of us are still without the new sort of role model Gwendolynn had been seeking, with only fairy tales to guide us, and only woodsmen to save us. At least in this story. But if you go back to the beginning and start over, there she is: Lynn of the first chapter. I still wonder why she ended up slipping into the mists instead of striding into the future.

There is no real ending here. Just an absolutely average, non-groundbreaking, reasonably satisfied, twenty-first century woman clinking shot glasses with male version of same.

"Everything happens for a reason," she declares bitterly.

"Bullshit." He answers.

They toss back their drinks.

Fade to black. Roll the credits.

~ ~ ~

IT'S NOT SO SIMPLE

Wynne

Sometimes I think that when the rain stops I will run away. The rain stops but I do not run. There is a meal to cook.

Which should I write about—the rain or the cooking?

The rain, of course, I have no control over. The cooking, barely more. The rain is a subject for poets, and I was one, once. The cooking, a topic for wives. Well, that decides it. I have been a wife five times over. Cooking wins 5 to 1. (Technically, I was only married to four of my five husbands, but that doesn't change anything.)

Most women with five husbands don't have to cook. Some celebs have more than five, but that's not the point. They have cooks, too. Whereas here, I am the cook, with perhaps as little control over what is in the pantry and how much, as how much water pours or drips from the sky. But, whatever he has provided, I must make something from it, quickly. That is, on time, so it is on the table when he comes.

The rain. I must, I can, make something of that as well. I promise myself that before this is done the rain will be a poem, poems. The roast is prose. Long, laborious prose. But I've learned how to do it. He will like it. He won't mock me.

I read over what I wrote. It sounds like I have five husbands all at once. I don't. Thank god! Imagine feeding them all. Absurd. But when I think about it, maybe I do. Have them, feed them all, all the time. The great, heavy weight of all of them crushes me at night. The unfillable chamber of their combined bellies is what I stoke, futilely, day after day. One husband, or five, equals all of the male species across all of time.

Here I am doing math again, and I was never good at it. Hence my domestic failures.

I chose this, I remind myself. I chose him. I chose each of them. I chose to leave when I had to. Except for the one I wanted, expected, to keep forever. Cancer took him from me. Dear god, I'm crying again. Like the rain, it never stops.

You know what? I'm leaving god out of this, going forward. God let me down with #3. Everything else was my own mistake.

"Going forward." That's an overused modern expression. The poet in me curls her lip. Remember how you hated that when you watched TV? And "at the end of the day." But, at the end of the day, I am still in the twenty-first century. I often forget.

Why have we reverted to such a primitive lifestyle? How did we end up re-enacting this classic division of labor? He builds, I bake. We thought we would be a team in a different way. Honestly, we just thought there would be less work. We each and together would flourish by removing ourselves from society. Everything would be simpler. Get real. It's a fight for survival out here.

Get real, girl. Your romantic notions about living closer to Nature are what got you here—on this useless, remote plot of land. And that creep's back-to-basics b.s. His "be free to be feminine" feminism and "I'm just a man-man" macho. He hit all your buttons and then, oh man, when he didn't disappoint in bed, wrapped you around his little finger. Got himself a little maid to keep out here in the pumpkin shell. Yeah, bad times.

So a genuine good guy shows up and helps get me out of my mess with #4, and blast it, now I have a #5. We just talked each other into it. Hell, I didn't trust romance anymore. And I couldn't go back to the city, or my family. Not in the state I was in. (Am in.) So I made the bargain. Like a job interview. I certainly had plenty of experience being a wife.

The rain makes you have to be honest with yourself. Okay, so say it:

Imagine what I've put myself through only for want of having a man who's good in the sack. If only I could have admitted how much the sex itself mattered, I wouldn't have fallen for all the other stuff—the flattery, the pretend interest, the surface things that add up to being compatible.

I <u>fell</u> for it? C'mon, be honest. I <u>demanded</u> it. Like I was taught. In spite of my modern attitudes, I demanded certain displays of affection and commitment before I jumped into bed with anyone. Should've taken them for the test run first. True, #3 might not have come my way, my soul mate.

But, be honest.

No, don't.

Anyway, I feel like #5 should be a keeper.

What I wanted was to be worshipped. Not in the sex goddess kind of way, but for my ability, for my potential. You know, like a son. Sons are worshipped. The red carpet rolls out for them. They are given every advantage, indulged, given leeway, sustained by the work of others so their destiny may be fulfilled. Daughters are raised to be sustainers, not sustainees. We are on a pedestal, sure—going nowhere.

I don't know. No one's that special, I guess. Sons turn into working stiffs, most of them, or cannon fodder. Maybe it's worse to be worshipped early on and then kicked around. Point is, I'll never know. I was put in my place early on.

I might have been a mystic or an inventor or just a good poet, painter or philosopher. For instance: I was so fed up with the rain today that I stripped the bed and myself and went naked out to the clothesline and hung out the sheets to be washed by the rain. It was cold, but worth it. Evan asked what I'd do if the sun didn't come out to dry them. I told him I'd put them in the oven. He thought that was funny, because we'd been rationing the wood, drying it out as fast as we can, which is not that fast. I said we'd better pray for the sun to come out, and told him to come help me do the sun dance. And he did. Got naked and we danced around in the mud. And don't you know that within a few hours the sun was out, hot and bright as anything, and we'll be sleeping on clean sheets tonight.

Not a word of that is true, but I do think the rain is letting up.

It seems to me that the real complaint here (me and the five husbands) is not their failure to worship me, but my ingrained tendency to worship them. So it is with the needy and their gods.

I wonder what has gotten into me today.

That was just wishful thinking about the rain. But I was prescient in any case.

Nancy.

How she has dissected me. It's true that while everyone has gone forward I have gone backward. And I do not advise it. Nancy is absolutely right on that score.

Other scores, however, need to be settled.

Nancy, you cannot believe what a fury you have stirred up here. One second I'm happily sitting here in my little leaky shack in the bayou, crying into my chicory tea (god, I hate the coffee here—oops, sorry, god's in the doghouse) because I'm thinking about writing a poem about rain, and anything to do with poetry gets me thinking about Philip, not to mention the rain—and I'm just having a swell, <u>tres</u> artistic time—when my new husband hurls himself through the front door, drenched, raging, flings a thick packet onto the table (slosh goes my so-called coffee to join his muddy puddles seeping between the floorboards), and bellows,

"She calls me a caveman!"

Well, how could I not laugh? How could he not laugh? But in the next minute we were at each other's throats because—he'd opened and read my mail, dammit! That opened the floodgates (like we're not already under water here). And the worst part is, he had read your treatise, and I had not! Can you believe that? He sat in his truck in the rain outside the post office, opened your thing, read it, tore home through the monsoon like a maniac, and threw the book at me. Literally.

Well, we had at it for a while (and no, there is no physical abuse here with Evan, so just put that out of your mind) and then we went to our separate corners, and I read it. And I read it again. What do you call this? A novella? Too short. Why did you send it? For a critique? For an ending? I suppose it's not bad, but prose was never my thing. I mean, where do you start (Brigadoon, really?) and where do you stop? (not where you did). The travelogues suited me, vignettes: I came to wherever, I saw wherever, I conquered wherever, and I left. For probing the depths I chose poetry. Used to. Or formless journaling. Scribbling helps me sort things out.

What you wrote about me and Philip disturbs me. What Rhiannon told you. It makes me wonder what was real. I could live without that.

I talked things over with Evan, of course. Evan is not a caveman. Our rescue was mutual. Why don't I start there, with the true tale of Evan, my hero. He was a victim too.

Bluebeard (good one, Nancy) was a total predator. He figured out my real identity pretty quickly and wooed me for my money, and I guess my body too, but it wasn't long before he went from being an exciting lover to being very emotionally cruel, holding out, making me feel like I was a screw-up, wasn't worthy. And I was a screw-up, not at all prepared for country life, or being left alone out here so much of the time. He isolated me, and basically treated me like a hostage, and I thank you for not putting more of what I did share with you into your saga, because that was before it got really bad, and I sure as hell am not telling you anything more about it now. No, it shall not be written.

Black Bart (that's what I call him) had this land scheme going, a very promising venture according to him: He and his pal would be setting up a little shop and curio place, "a roadside attraction, if you will," in the vicinity of a to-be off-ramp for a to-be upscale development on a (to-be?) scenic stretch of road that goes pretty much nowhere except to a swampy nature preserve. The men were rehabbing an old storage structure on the rise near the roadway for the business; and there would be a caretaker home, eventually a small community of homes ("a collective, if you will") down the hill a ways. Currently there was a single ramshackle farmhouse, where Bart stayed when he wasn't on the road rounding up investors and cajoling credit out of suppliers. He skimmed off as much as he could from any actual pay-ins and used the credit to get the tools and materials Evan needed when he came out on weekends to work on the retail space. Evan was a local, like Bart and the others. They'd had their shot out in the world seeking better opportunities, some making out pretty well (not Evan—artist, carpenter), yet still they longed for their swath of swampland.

Weird how this country gets in your blood. It's more like a mood than a landscape. Misty, no hard edges. A waking drizzly dream in which sunshine may eject from the heavens at any moment to cast a celestial spotlight on—oh look, it's not hell on earth, it's Eden! Then you stick around to see it happen again. (Kind of like when you have sex that's totally, exquisitely satisfying with an otherwise inattentive partner, and you wonder if it was a fluke, or your own private dream, or if it could possibly be repeated, and you tough it out with someone who generally does not make you feel all that good to see if maybe heaven's actually always there waiting behind the clouds, even loving you through the clouds, and the problem is not the sky but you.)

The point is, one's reason blurs here like the fog-shrouded horizon. If you're a transplant like me. As for the natives, I suppose they are addled practically from birth. Not only had some of Bart's cohorts made super good lives for themselves out in the world, which they were willing to give up for this collective in a roadside gully, but they were willing to pitch in with a guy whose bad behavior they knew well. Didn't matter. He was a homie, he was pushing a dream, pushing their buttons. Like he pushed mine. You know this part—he picked up on what I was writing on my blog about living in nature, finding one's authentic nature. One of my posts was a reminiscence about summers with my grandparents on the bayou. Once he caught that whiff of Louisiana in my on-line opus I was doomed. How easy it was for him to uncover my identity and then woo me out here to homestead with him. How easy it was for him to track down anything I'd published or put on-line—those crappy poems, as well as some really thoughtful, heartfelt feminist confessionals—so that when I got to him, though he wasn't quite so attractive in person as in his photos, he seemed to anticipate my every need. That was some game he played.

(She tries to sound breezy and philosophical about it, but her hands are shaking and a wave of nausea rises at the memories, the memories of what she thought was happening overlaid with the knowledge of what he was really doing, plotting.)

Humiliation literally gets stuck in the craw. There is very little that comes up or goes down that does not have to push past.

Try again.

The hitch in Bart's scam was Evan. Evan wanted badly to come back to the boonies to live a simple life and devote himself to painting. He didn't have much money to invest, but he committed his labor, and he couldn't wait to start fixing up the buildings. He was up on the hill almost every weekend, camping out in the giant shed as he rebuilt and customized it for our roadside attraction. That was after he'd finally browbeaten Bart into seeing to the utility hookups, an effort that came back to haunt him. It was the cut-off notices and unpaid supplier bills that brought Evan storming down to our hovel looking for Bart. I hadn't seen my husband in days, and despite being essentially trapped in a leaky shack without a lot of provisions, I wasn't missing him. (Bluebeard might actually have been trying to kill me, he sabotaged my car before he left.)

So Evan found me in my pumpkin shell, not being kept well at all. We started going through the bills. Then looking for anything Bart had in writing about the property and improvements. I was supposed to have copies of all of that. Black Bart had taken it all. And he took my journals and he took my poems, the few I had written, my letters from you and my family, everything. A panic started building up in me, a panic I couldn't let Evan see, at how I had been played, how Bart had been able to play me for such a fool. I just focused my attention on the real estate problem, my living situation, and how quickly I could get a restraining order and a divorce.

Evan was more angry at my situation than his own. Evan was righteous. Evan had boundless energy. What he didn't have was boundless credit. He was ready to aid my escape, but I was too broken to go anywhere, and he was too broke to do much more than drive me to the bus. Besides, my desire to come out to this place had been sincere. I had stayed so far, hadn't I? Even when I had my chances to leave, even when my instincts screamed at me to leave. But now I just wasn't fit for society.

A lot of shit went down. Legal, personal. The collective, such as it was, shattered. Everyone had had enough of Bart and his schemes. I was an outsider, I had been stupid enough to marry the jerk, I had signed off on his notes. I was distrusted and pitied and shunned. Or maybe that's just what humiliated people think people think about them. I suppose they were ashamed of themselves for not keeping a closer eye on Bart, and for being suckered themselves. Evan just clung to his dream. He was honorable. Every one of us looked to him for leadership and felt that if we could help him see his dream through, our roles in the mess would be redeemed. Everyone but me worked out a deal to transfer their shares to Evan. I offered to stay on as a business partner. I still had some money Bart couldn't get at. Evan could give up his job and his place in town and move into the house with me—good guy that he is, he'd already put in a fair amount of work to make it more comfortable. With a decent place to stay and someone helping out, he could make more progress on the other building. We struck our deal, and after a while we struck a couple of others. Evan was the one who brought up "friends with benefits" and then I was the one who proposed.

I was not really so "well set financially" when Philip died, by the way. Are you kidding? My husband was a poetry professor. The children inherited. I got the house. I don't think I need elaborate on how I burned through a good deal of the money after I'd sold it. And now I'm burning through the rest. I wonder how long we can hold out.

The venture here is not going to make it. Not only did the plan hinge on way too many ifs from the start (how many ifs does it take to go from worth-a-try to wishful-thinking?), but Evan and I are in no way fit or committed enough to carry it through. I'm supposed to be making crafts and decorations and signs and such for the shop, work up some more recycled t-shirts and other novelties. My assignments are only those things I've volunteered for, yet I sit here writing most of the day, and I'd been doing so even before "Making the Worst of Things" dropped (so to speak). I was trying to get the poetry back. But now I have to do this.

And Evan. He's a painter. Got out of school and moved to the city like we all do. New Orleans was his Big Apple.

Got in on the boom times when there was lots of work for guys with mechanical and carpentry skills, from rehabbing decaying old row houses into shops and yuppie bars to putting up huge new high-rises where whole blocks had been razed. Sometimes he lucked into a commission or a great studio space. So he had what it took to get the shop and this little cottage shaped up, but now that he's out here full time, and I'm putting meals on the table—

Yeah, it's pretty clear that he's turned the roadside attraction into a painting studio. He stopped trying to hide it, like I stopped trying to hide my writing. He is not installing shelves and display counters, just as I'm not making the merchandise to fill them. We're each doing our own thing. It's kind of awesome. But it can't go on. The exit ramp to nowhere from the road to nowhere is going nowhere. Folks and their businesses are pulling out of this area not moving in. Not that it's anything to you, Nancy, but I'm pretty sure Evan knows this and doesn't want to admit it. And I'm also pretty sure he's reading this, so now I have admitted it for him.

What happened was, I forgave Evan for reading "The Worst" before I had even seen it. I was kind of (kind of) glad he had, because it saved me from deciding if I should show him or hide it. And he apologized. Profusely. He said that he thought he was opening a reply to some manuscript I'd sent out, that he expected it to be something I had written, but he wasn't so interested in reading my stuff—he said—but the response to it. To see if I was trying to leave him. Well, that confession led to an interesting conversation about why he would put together my sending out manuscripts (if I had been doing so) with my leaving him. And I was finding him very dear, and felt eager to assure him that I was really committed to our marriage, when he comes out with this:

"Do you really feel like I mock you?"

I was dumbfounded. I don't know how long it took me to form the words, "Have you been reading my journal?"

It took him even longer to answer, and the whole time our eyes were locked in a staring contest.

"No."

No. He said no. Looked right into my eyes and said, "No."

It wasn't like he was lying to me. He was telling me a lot. How much he didn't want to hurt me. I didn't want to hurt him either. I could've killed him then, because it made me mad as hell that he should read something in my journal and be hurt by it and now it was me who had to apologize. I mean, my head was going to explode, and he was just staring into my eyes, willing me to go as passive as he had.

So I said, as casually as I could, "Because it might be disturbing to read my journals. The way I drift into fantasy sometimes. And sometimes, sitting right here at this table, I forget, you know. That it's you and not him who will be coming through that door. And then I start writing like I'm still back there. Only I shouldn't have written anything then, when I was with Bart. I know that now. He would spy out everything that was mine, that was just for me, and find a way to toy with me, to use whatever he knew or suspected against me. You know that first day, when we went looking for paperwork? There was more missing than I said. That asshole took all my writing, all my letters—those he'd let me have."

I was getting pretty agitated thinking about it. Evan looked really ashamed. Hard to say who was more uncomfortable. End of staring contest.

Evan: "I wish I could have saved you from him."

Me: "You did."

Him: "Not soon enough."

Me: "I wonder why I stuck around and took the abuse for so long, didn't stick up for myself. Was I waiting for you? I feel like we're meant to be together. You know, everything happens for a reason." (And f. you, Nancy.)

Him: "I'm glad you see it that way, if you really do."

Me: "I do."

Him: "I do."

Me (at his expression): "What?"

Him: "We just got married again."

Me: "I mean it, Evan. I've meant it from the start."

The fact is, we have never yet said "I love you" to each other. Not that it couldn't happen. I think we don't want it to be gratuitous. And you know what? He doesn't have to love me. He's interested in me. He's here for me.

He said: "You leave your journals and papers out where I could look if I wanted to. So, I wonder if you want me to look. Or if you're testing me. To see if you can trust me."

"Yes, I'm testing you." There, I admitted it. "Because I really need to trust you. If I even suspected you were not to be trusted I would have to leave, and I don't want to leave."

"You can trust me never to use your art against you, Wynne."

I almost told him then that I loved him, but I showed him instead.

Yes, Nancy, my fifth husband is the rugged type. Fit and physical. He pleases me a lot with his forthright enthusiasm for sex. His lovemaking is not complicated or tentative or manipulative or lacking in affection. Not needy or overbearing or self-conscious. He is present. He is happy with my presence. He expects and desires nothing more or less from me. He is healing me. I think he fears that once I am healed I will leave. I get the sense it has happened before, and that's why his pals distrust me. They don't understand. I hope they never do.

Evan asked me if I was writing a response to you. I said yes, but no. I was writing answers to you I was unlikely to send. I offered to send a short note just to let you know I had not married a caveman, but he said not to bother about defending his honor. Still, he thought I might benefit from addressing what you have written about "the others." We both knew he didn't mean Bart. We will say no more about Bart. In fact Evan suggested we switch living arrangements. He can use this place, so full of awful memories for me, as his painting studio. We can live up by the road in the "gallery," such as it is, where he says it will be easier to "assess our situation" and formulate a plan. I'm not sure how far he read in this journal, or if he has been thinking along the same lines as me. But now we're talking. We need to decide what to do, together.

I don't concern myself about his reading this now, because I take care to put my writing away. Not hidden, but with my personal things, out of respect for him. We will be communicating directly and not through these pages.

Not that it undoes what he has read in your little parable, Nancy. Thus his challenge to me to consider what you said about Philip, David and Joel. To be honest, I'd nearly forgotten David and Joel. Each in his way is like a bright fairy-tale dream. I awoke with pleasant memories and a twinge of regret. Why could I not dream on? Thanks for reminding me about them, I guess.

Then there's Philip. I suppose I have to have a long think about Philip now.

Damn. I did not need this, Nancy. This doubting of the very core of my life, my prime of life, my longest relationship, which encompassed both motherhood and widowhood. No, I do not need this. Why besmirch my memories of Philip? Why? And I was finally writing poetry again.

Dear Nancy, I have made the same mistake four, and maybe five times, and you nailed the reason why: I insist on remaking myself. I really try to, am willing to. I didn't give up on writing the new story of the new woman—no, the authentic woman. No. "The True Story of an Authentic Woman"—that's it.

I did not give up on it, I tried to live it. I realized that I was not, could never be, that woman without a reboot of some kind, an attitude adjustment. A fresh start. The first start (boss daddy, weepy mommy, spoiled brothers) hadn't been ideal. I kept remaking myself, starting again. Only in doing so, I somehow ended up in reverse. You called it, Nancy.

My mistake with the men was supposing they could start over too, that they wanted to. You know, we were attracted, so I thought that meant we were the same on a deeper level. Well, what we shared was desire, which may be constant enough (if you don't stick around too long, although you never know how long you have), but the men did not share in my new-leaf approach to life. I see that you don't either, Nancy. And thanks to you, I see that it could be rather rare, or rarely acted upon so thoroughly or frequently as in my own case.

I was a fool to think #s 1, 2, 3 and 4 would be all new-leafy like me. I mean, in each case (in every case, Nancy, including Joel), some old pal of my new beau would drop a hint about his past life, and I would totally dismiss it. Who was I to get hung up on past lives? I may have appeared to be re-enacting a familiar role, but to my mind my men and I were always equals: I was starting over, they were starting over.

Their friends tried to tell me. Every time.

Joel: You think I was surprised to learn about the boyfriend? Not. God, I loved Joel. (There I go again with god, dammit.) Joel was a joy to talk to and a doll to live with. (Do you sense there was something he wasn't?)

David: Doh! Ray had him pegged in one sniff, but I'd already heard it all from the Paris crowd. (I am very happy about you and Ray, by the way. Maybe you two are the authentic new-way and don't even know it.)

(Huh, maybe it's excess self-consciousness that kills authenticity. Discuss.)

Philip:

Sorry. Stalled out.

Philip. Evan is also probing now. He's trying to encourage me to stick with poetry. He's asked to see some of the poems I've been writing.

I told him I would show him the poetry if he would show me the paintings. He's been very secretive about them as we switch domiciles. He says he doesn't want me to see them unfinished. He promises to hang the finished ones, if I can live with them. What does that mean? They are drying in a back room and I'm not allowed to look. Anyway, I've seen enough of Evan's work to know that the paintings will be good paintings. Can't say if I'll like them. Pretty sure he won't like my poetry, what there is of it. I keep rewriting the same things over and over.

Philip. I was warned about him too, Nancy, not that I hadn't already experienced the full treatment by that time: Teacher's pet for a semester, emphasis on the pet, but not until after he'd teased me and taunted me through my B+.

Yeah, B+. He wasn't punishing me because I didn't put out. He really didn't think I deserved an A, and he was right. You and Rhiannon were right. He used me and my poetry for his own purposes, one of which was sexual and one of which was ego. No one was allowed to surpass him or make him passé, no woman certainly, and he sabotaged the voices that were strongest. Don't think I didn't notice. But I was turned on by his game also. I wasn't writing poetry, I was giving him what he wanted and trying to make him lose his cool. Somehow we made it through my B+ and commenced an A+ affair. I did not consider myself his victim. He was a very good husband, and raising his children was a real achievement and a true joy. We were happy, Nancy. You saw that. I was happy.

"He was an older man, nice looking, not condescending that I could tell, and not smarmy. But he sure had our Lynn—his Gwendolynn—in his thrall. She positively worshipped him, and he absolutely loved that about her and rewarded her for it."

I am speechless at this.

The man's poetry was astonishing, I thought so then and I think so now. He didn't have to worry about me or any of his students surpassing him. No one will ever surpass him, he was the best of his generation.

That said, every generation is destined to be blown off by the next. It was pointless for Philip to defend his mountaintop. No one was coming to unseat him, we were looking to scale other summits. His star was dimming, his steeped-in-the-classics poetry losing its shine along with the classics themselves, those monuments to patriarchal elitism. But that doesn't change the fact that Philip did write for everyone. His poems were messages to all humanity written in the only language he knew. Sex and its euphemisms through the ages are part of the lexicon. He liked teaching those. He liked leading unsuspecting students through a metaphorical tour of human anatomy. "And what else might the rose represent in this case, the glistening dewy pink bud trembling to open?"

You get the idea.

And then we would write similar stuff back at him, sometimes mocking, sometimes because we desperately wanted to make it as poets and had been convinced that the process of unleashing sexual energy was required, a letting-go, in order for one's true artistic talent to flow. Philip admired the spoofs as much as the sincere attempts, and retained a rather stimulating set of student-written soft porn for his own pleasure. I found it. None of my poems were among the collection. I like to think that was out of respect for me, but those poems he held onto really were superior to my passive-aggressive attempts.

I shredded all of it. I actually knew many of those former students or had known them as students. There were a few women I wanted to apologize to, perhaps some who owed an apology to me. How far had Philip taken things with them? And as his wife, why could I not have sated his desires and protected them from him?

That's what they must have thought. But Philip and I did satisfy each other physically. Only, Philip was wired for words. There was a way in which only the words could turn him on. Did some of these students' words turn him on enough to act on them? Really, I feel more sorry for the other women than for myself. Philip, my dear husband, was a pleasure to romp with, but he was never going to live up to the sort of erotica he was laying on those wishful women. (I have found only scraps of his poems to them, in the margins or quoted in the poems back to him.) What were they thinking?

Anyway, once we fell in love and married, I no longer played those games with Philip and he did not expect me to. Whether he expected me to give up writing poetry entirely, or realized I had, I do not know. I think we both felt immersed in poetry because I became an important sounding board for his serious stuff. He sought my opinion and often followed my advice (not in the moment, when he could be defensive; but later I would see my impact in the final version). Philip made me feel like his poetry was my poetry. And he made me feel loved, and I have no reason to think he didn't love me for being me. You're the one who's making the worst of things, Nancy. In fact you got the story of me and Philip completely wrong. This is how it should go:

"He was an older man, nice looking. He was condescending, he was smarmy. But he was always gallant to his lady-love Gwendolynn. She stood shoulder-to-shoulder with him as wife and creative partner, and they loved each other deeply."

Queen of the Round Table—I laugh now (bitterly). Set myself up to need a circle, a posse. That is not a good thing in grad school, as it turns out. Posses are more like piranhas in an MFA program. And it's not the same as in the academic departments, where the preferred method of getting a leg up is cheating. Fudging lab results. Hacking exam files. No, when it comes to the expressive arts, the game is all about psyching-out, undermining confidence, diverting energy. Behold the critique group. Not my loyal swains. Not my private pep club. Egotistical and envious. And once I was openly in a relationship with Philip? They killed with kindness.

When I think back on some of the crap "critique" that was laid on me, it almost makes me angrier than what Bart did. That was private—sicko meets sucker. He didn't pretend he was looking out for me. I had indentured myself to him. He let me know that. (I know, it doesn't make any sense. I guess it comes down to pride. A person will put up with a lot just to put off admitting a mistake, to the world or oneself.)

But the critique group—sharks, I tell you. Some of them might try to be helpful—but what the hell do they know? Their own taste? What's politically popular? What gets awards? Prose: They scoff at bestsellers—lowbrow stuff. True art must be more edgy, more provocative, more personal. More more more personal. Oh, but please, not so emotional! (This is how women are silenced. If the artistry of the work can be disputed, the content may be dismissed.) And poetry? If you haven't taken apart the very alphabet and put it back together inside-out, then, my dear, you have produced sentimental doggerel. Back to the drawing board you go, trying desperately not to lose the coherence of the original idea while you dismantle and reconstruct its parts. Instead of chiseling a form from marble you're stacking up bricks, brutal and rough around the edges.

Philip never espoused such party tricks. That's why he was on his way out. Not that the classical line is necessarily any easier to decipher—not to the modern ear—but his objective was to preserve the language, not to break it. Still, when I complained about the critique groups, Philip told me it was important to listen and to be open to criticism. Well, serious artists must suffer, I'm told, and the critique group was always there to help.

I suppose that by not coming to my defense Philip was complicit in the breaking down of my ego, but that project had been underway ever since I can remember. Call it a community project. Philip was just Authority epitomized, dressed in its best suit.

Let's face it, every single thing a woman does is judged by male standards if not by men themselves. The need to ask permission of an authority figure—in my day, always a male—is instilled in girls early. If we were lucky enough to miss some of those lessons, society surely took pains to indoctrinate us as soon as we got into the mix.

Once I had switched from student to wife, from ingenue to den mother, I saw clearly how this works in the university setting, where the undermining of a woman's confidence is nowhere greater than in the arts. Oh, I know that girls have typically been left out of science, math, engineering (all that "brainy" stuff) but once we got a foot in the door, achievements followed. Recognition might be belated, but the work stands on its own merits in a measurable realm. Not so in the fine arts, where creativity by definition is a venture into the unknown, the not-yet-done, never-before-seen. But somehow, whenever a woman strays too far into the avant-garde, her work is <u>too</u> new, too foreign, too far off the beaten path. For the very traits by which a man's art is judged brilliant, a woman's is decried as immature, unrefined, or possibly "too ambitious."

What offends me most, thinking back to my stint in academia, is not the sexism, but the gamesmanship. Everyone was on the make. Art was a side racket. I had been around the world, built and sold a business, loved and lost twice (or so) yet I was totally unprepared for the head trips and political maneuvers of grad school. The gossip about me was as vulgar and mean as you can imagine—bad poet bags prof—but I felt like I came out ahead. The degree felt hollow. Philip was my life.

Now I am going to write about sex and power and desire and need. Nancy puts all this in terms of gender roles, evolved and devolved. I was enlightened and now I've fallen back. I was liberated and now I'm less so. But is it really so unenlightened to come to the conclusion that I don't need a man in my head (even the well-intentioned ones will screw you up), I just need a good man in my bed? Someone to be naked with, really naked. Who looks at you and holds you in a way that lets you know you're real, and you're okay.

When we're young, we're really confused. That is, we're horny, and all screwed up by a culture in which the chase is everything. There is a hunt on one side, entrapment on the other. ("I chased her until she caught me," the old saw goes.) It's a competition. Who gets the apple? Who gets the cherry? Or the banana? Before or after satisfying our sexual attraction, we are supposed to become soulmates, and then, after tying the knot, workmates—so that after the entire universe has conspired to make sex the most obvious and important attractor, it is expected to be secondary.

Historically, the only sexual satisfaction guaranteed by marriage is the man's. Practically speaking, there are many marriages and phases of marriage in which both partners are too tuckered out from the daily grind to do any grinding at night. So, it is important to have more points of connection than the erogenous zones; but expectations are expectations, and marriage provides a very long stretch in which one or both partners may feel a little or a lot unfulfilled. And that's if you're lucky in love.

Sex and power. How often are women depicted as being teases, as withholding or using sex to get what we want? What I find ironic is that men do the same thing, only <u>they'll</u> do so <u>knowing</u> that they can't actually deliver the satisfaction the woman craves, but what they can do is make her ashamed, as though it's her fault, so she won't speak of it, and then they are free to please themselves.

Wives must be content to indulge ourselves with shopping, travel, spas, home decor, fashion and food. The food comes closest to our true hunger for contact, touch, warmth—the roiling thrill and deep-ocean, suspended-consciousness state of sexual pleasure. Like the archetypal southern belle, we may eat demurely in public (today we call it "healthy eating") then feed our hunger and our guilty cravings in private. It's not that sexual appetite is taboo for a woman. It's encouraged. We are supposed to want some guy enough to be obsessed with pleasing him. This is the same for men in the courtship phase, possibly extending to honeymoon. Then the paths diverge. He is entitled to want as much as he wants. She is expected to be pleased with whatever she gets.

I keep framing this in terms of traditional gender roles, but those roles are gradually losing their grip on us. Yet the issues of sex and power remain, of hunger and desire, of relationships public and private. "It takes two to tangle," Grannie used to say. To which Gramps would say, "Tango, dear. It's Tango!" And then he'd swoop in and dance her around the room, ending with a deep dip while she giggled like a girl.

All the rest of the time they were at each other's throats, as I recall.

I was working my way back to Joel. The balance of power and desire. I was the man in that relationship, put in traditional terms. I had the power. I had the desire that powered our relationship. I was the one who was most demanding and least content. The sex didn't matter as much to him. Thinking back now from this perspective, he was not the one I could "get naked with and feel okay." We were much more okay in clothes, playing dress-up in public, or each of us dressing and doing as we pleased in our his-'n-her flat. We took care of each other, respected each other, but nothing could overcome my neediness. My neediness, that's how I thought of it. But pretty obviously Joel's needs weren't being met either. I don't doubt he felt just as guilty about it as I did.

When you love someone you feel like you shouldn't be putting so much stock in the sexual satisfaction or dissatisfaction of the moment. There's a whole lifetime to consider, two whole people who are a lot more than their libidos. I've said it myself, to myself: Not being entirely replete is hardly the same as starving. There is so much more to share and enjoy with your soulmate than sex. And I have known many happy (happier than me) single people. They are either not looking at all, or they are holding out—wisely calculating that no mate is better than the wrong mate. As for me, I came to feel that it was easier on my soul to abstain than to feel not quite entirely satisfied. The hunger goes away if you don't feed it at all. You move on to other interests. When Philip gave up on sex, I was happy to do so as well.

Joel, though. I couldn't have a platonic relationship with him, not at that age, not when I found him so beautiful. I was the aggressor. He was compliant. And not satisfied.

I had to have David to assure myself I was still a turn-on to men, not just by "catching" him, but by being out and about with him in flattering places, with flattering people. (In places that flattered me, with people who were attracted to me.)

Philip was just right. I felt like Goldilocks when we finally got together. He had the sophistication of David's crowd (not to mention more brains and social conscience) but the solidity of my liquid lunch buddies—"the

Dads"—he <u>was</u> a Dad! And he was a true romantic and devotee of womanly beauty. He lavished attention and affection on me.

I was a happy, busy, tired wife and mother, and it never occurred to me to want more than what he gave me. But then came the time when the kids were often away. I segued from more-mother to more-wife—on his arm, assisting his work. I expected more passion but got less. On one level, we were actually relieved when we learned how sick he was.

Mother, wife, secretary, nurse. Same ol', same ol', right, Nancy? Is there any alternative? What are we supposed to do, turn into plants? I loved Philip and I nursed him to the end. The selflessness was good for me. But I knew what was coming, so why didn't I prepare myself better? I think I was exhausted. That's about the only thing I remember for a long stretch. Not what I did, just how tired I was. For a time, I didn't give a thought to sex or poetry or the future.

Wife, nurse, then widow. I was single again. I just assumed I knew how to protect myself. I had made sure early on to learn how to defend myself against physical attack. Whoever it was, I always felt like if it came to blows, "I could take him" (or her). And I was firm in my resolve that should violence ever transpire, I would be out of there. One strike and you're out, fella. Bart knew better than to lay a finger on me in anger. If only he had. I had no idea what kind of emotional abuse a man could cook up intentionally. I was completely unprepared for his level of malice.

But the sad truth is this: it was the entrenched but benign imbalance of power between me and Philip that softened me up for Bart. My adulation of my husband, my feeling of emptiness without him. I'd already lost myself, but I didn't know this until it was too late. And how could Philip have anticipated any of this? If he was setting me up, it was only to be his devoted wife to the end of his days. It's just that the end came too soon. I still had a sex drive waiting to be relit.

By the way, there is a huge hole in your thesis, Nancy. An incomplete premise. That I was an evolved creature who went backwards. You point out that I kept remaking myself. And so? Who was Lynn, your modern, liberated friend? Wynne is so much closer to my authentic self than Lynn. Authentic in the sense of original. They called me Winnie back in Tulsa, don't you know. Like the neighing of a horse. Certainly not like a winner. I was not a winner,

I was a wanter—who didn't get a lot of what she wanted.

Well, that's a growing-up thing. We assess our assets and decide what's attainable. Positive and negative role models are a big influence. I loved my mom, but I didn't want to be her. Or be near her, by the time I reached puberty—she did not approve of the way I "blossomed" and was on constant alert for my virginity. I loved my dad, but I never wanted to be with a man like him. He commanded respect and doled out affection in minuscule portions. Now there's a thought: Mother was all love and no respect, father was all respect and no love. I intended to be both respected and loved.

I found myself, my self-confidence, my fun and creative side, in Lynn. Lynn wasn't a put-on, none of my personas were. (All one in here, last I checked, in spite of Bart trying to break my mind.) I saw the world as a costume party and played my different characters to suit the conditions.

Right, that's it: What are the conditions in which we grow best? City life? World travel? Family focus? Out in the boonies? Alone? Partnered? These things change as we change. If we have found that place in which to grow—and have grown—then the desire to move on may actually be inevitable in order for the personal experiment to continue. (And if we failed, and put ourselves in a worse position, then moving on is an absolute necessity.)

Lynn was a supergirl I imagined and briefly embodied. Gwen too. But fictions only go so deep. Below the surface, always, just li'l ol' me. I didn't want to be my mom, or marry a man like my dad, but I did (do) want to be a woman, to fully discover myself as a human, as a woman, as an individual. And dammit, for me anyway, that doesn't seem to be possible, fully possible—even the being-an-individual part—without the complimentary, often incendiary presence of a man.

Primitive? I call it natural. That is the pure honest truth about me, and in no way imposes the same truth on anyone else. I'm really sorry I can't be anyone's missing link. I sure as hell never signed up to be a foot soldier or poster child for any cause. I've come back to Louisiana, where I used to sit and listen to bugs and frogs and birds, watch sun and shadow play across the horizon, daydream and imagine. If only someone had given me a pen and pad back then, the poems I could have written. But at least I was allowed to roam free. My grandparents' home, overflowing with family in summertime, was full of squabbling. It made me laugh. It felt human, the quarrels like clouds chasing across the sky. Not like the unnatural silence of my parents' house, where dad always won. He shouted, she cried, game over. I went to that place with Bart, so help me, and when I saw where I was I started climbing out, fighting back. It wasn't such a good strategy. Mom probably tried it early on, and early on got her comeuppance.

These are things I wish I didn't have to think about again, Nancy. I didn't come out here to solve the gender problem. I came here to find those poems I left unwritten out under the oak tree (right, there is not an oak tree within ten miles of this place), that penned themselves against the white mists, that sprang up between the attic floorboards to sift into my dreams while the grown-up voices murmured below and my cousins snored in their cots on either side of mine. From there I would work my way to the poetry I had in mind to write back when I went for my MFA. How ironic that I fell in love with my poetry teacher and then dropped poetry for all those years. But I wasn't entirely stalled out. Philip taught me everything I need to know about poetry. The rest has been me learning about myself.

It's cold in here. This little burp of land is drier but way windier than where the old house, now studio, is situated down the hill. And this building wasn't intended to be lived in like we're living in it. The front rooms that have decent light are big and drafty. Small rooms in the back for office and storage can be made warmer with space heaters, but they've become claustrophobic, crowded with our stuff. We sit out here next to the old stove that was put in for atmosphere, with a collection of rustic furniture and curios taking shape around us (we're still pushing toward the roadside attraction idea, dreamers that we are), and it's like we're in a wax museum display of country life.

I can see the problems ahead. We have been thrown together. Not randomly, exactly. More like a couple of odd pieces of debris that tides and time bring into proximity of one another, and some feature of each results in an entanglement that ultimately, although random, seems inevitable. There is an arranged-marriage quality to our union. That yenta Fate brought us together; we wed in good faith, we expect to make it work, to find a place on the continuum of tolerance-to-love while joining together in a partnership of survival.

You may find that primitive, Nancy, our surrender to circumstance, but what isn't random when you get right down to it? You and Ray fell in love, like you were made for each other. But it was happenstance that brought you into each other's orbits, and some quirk of each that led to something like a good fit. Still, like a puzzle piece with a knob here and a jog there, each of us has multiple options for fitting to another, and I don't mean body parts.

Is it the who or the when that makes a relationship? Is it the you or the me? How patient can we each be? I see myself being content in this relationship the way I was with Philip, but not because I am content with Evan. (I am now, but I don't expect to be quite as much in the future, when we have to face up to our financial problems, when he goes off to paint in his studio or sell art in the city.) No, we will have the usual complications. But I'm content with myself. I can keep my own interests in the forefront. The man is necessary, just speaking for myself. But the more I denied it (Nancy would call this being modern, liberated) and the more I fought it, the less contentment I found.

I guess that goes without saying. Fighting is the opposite of contentment. More though, my taste was distorted. That wave I rode was going farther and farther from where I started, from what I wanted, what I dreamed of. I found partners to ride the tides with, and honestly, we did fit in some or many ways. I could have ridden along with any of them, I think, if only I could have embraced the idea of that random-arranged union one learns to function within, without surrendering oneself.

"The man is necessary"—a little nugget of pure truth glitters out of my stream of words. Again, speaking just personally (sheesh, I have to apologize for this?), it's the male partner I crave. My sexuality may be bi, but my psyche is not so fluid. Regardless of having zero urge to bear children, regardless of growing from tomboy to amazon woman with barely a nod to frilliness and traditional femininity, I feel myself to be a woman through and through. And what a man brings me, strangely—(wow, Nancy, think about it: strangely, because we always complain about not being understood) —what a man brings me is the guarantee of separateness, of the privacy afforded by his psyche being so inherently different from mine. His foreignness attracts me. It comforts me. I would hate for everyone to be like me, to feel like me, to care and create like me—what torment. He is different. I can marvel at him. I don't have to be in there with him, and the poor man need not be in here with me. (Bart trespassed, but even he could not conquer this place.) By being fundamentally incomprehensible to each other, male and female preserve their autonomy even in the closest relationship. (What do you think, Nancy? Isn't that you and Ray?)

The man is an attachment that fits and makes me stronger, but also an irritant that hardens and defines. He is not dispensable. I could split right now, shake off this arranged-random liaison, and set forth as an independent woman, free and unfettered. Right. And how long would it be before I was on the prowl again, or again hungry and ready to take the bait? I should hope that I have gained in strength and self-knowledge enough to avoid the bad matches, that I would go it alone before I fell in with the wrong guy again. But this wouldn't change the notion, the desire, to have a man in my life.

The man is necessary. And thus, to some extent, interchangeable. Isn't that exactly the attitude men have had about women through the ages? Doesn't that make my proclivity to partnering actually advanced, in the sense of gender-equalized, and not regressed? Yes, I got hurt, used—but that was part of the game too, the stimulus of being both partners and adversaries, testing wills, testing sincerity. The game is always on because of that fundamental divide that keeps our natures and motives shielded from even the closest of soulmates.

Philip was not my adversary. I fell for him willingly. Followed him willingly. Was it so wrong to idolize him and serve him? Was he wrong to pamper me and protect me? Is the tug-of-war, the inner battle of whether to be one's own person or belong to another any nobler? Isn't it conceivable that <u>he</u> makes me more <u>me</u>?

It's not true that the women of the past, those nameless ones, provide inadequate role models. The more society stifled them, the more essential it was for them to find contentment within themselves, to not let circumstance defeat them. You could call their lives circumscribed, but also circumspect—self-contained. More than stoic. Proud and protective of the secret spark that none may ever know but she. Woman has always been a mystery behind a mask painted by others. I suppose we could debate whether such self-possession is healthy, or if perfect understanding between the genders is obtainable, or if there really is a biological difference such as I've described. Surely many of my experiences have been purely cultural.

I feel protective of the women of the past. I don't want to rebel against them or belittle their lives. They got us this far. Are we what they imagined we'd be? Now we want to imagine Future Woman. I'm not suggesting looking over our shoulders for her. Or even more deeply into ourselves. No, not that. I truly hope that she'll not be wasting so much of her life fighting herself or trying to prove a point. She'll become Future Woman simply by looking forward instead of casting around for approval.

I am not she. But I am myself. Still. Call me what you will. I've been celebrated, spoiled, tested and teased. Lately battered by rough seas. I feel worn so smooth that there's no resistance left in me, no more need. Want, yes. Wisdom, I hope. Poetry, pretty sure. Love, working on it.

I saw Evan's paintings. I am dismayed by what he has done with this boggy countryside. Now I look into the mist and see his strange scenes taking shape, mystical landscapes within landscapes. He is a lush, suggestive storyteller. My poems are more to the point. Sometimes I'm at risk of honing them down until there's nothing left. Anyway, there is no comparison. He may read them. He has shown me his soul. I told him I loved the paintings, but there was a little Freudian slip: "I love y... them."

He said, laughing, "I love... them too."

* Interlude *

Everyone in the Harlequin Club was leaning in to catch what was going on at the Round Table. Rhiannon had created a stir when she rushed in triumphantly clutching several copies of PoetryTrip.com's "Special Annual Deluxe

Print Issue," which she'd snapped up the minute they landed at the museum gift shop. She sent a couple copies around the table.

"Page sixteen, sixteen and seventeen, that's Gwendolynn, that's our Lynn!" Someone behind her cheered, and she handed a copy back to them before pushing into the booth. Clayford and Mateo were right behind her. They pulled up chairs to close the circle. Each had their own copy, Mateo sent his over to the bar with the server. A few people pushed back through the incoming Happy Hour throng to go look for more copies at the nearby news stand. Then an eerie silence fell over the busy establishment as people read poetry, first Gwendolynn's, and then sampling the rest of the journal in order to judge her poems by the company they kept.

Gradually the club returned to normal. Conversation resumed. Decibels increased. At the Round Table, Lynn's old friends expressed pleasure and relief at having this evidence of her continued existence, as well as grudging admiration for the poems.

"I do think they're good, but it's still pretty amazing she got published in PoetryTrip, the actual print issue, don't you think?"

"Oh no, not really. Don't forget who she was married

to before, you know, dropping out and shacking up with those mountain men." (That's how much they knew about Louisiana.)

The undercurrent of jealousy was becoming more palpable, alongside a suspicion that Lynn might have put one over on them or, alternatively, was really in trouble. The conflicting emotions drove them to drink more than usual. Tongues loosened. But the magazines kept circulating, and every so often one of those loyal swains of the Round Table would look up from the page and say quietly, "It's really very good. Good for Lynn."

Not a word of that is true. But Evan did say the poems were "damn fine." He thinks I should start sending them out, and keeps telling me to stop rewriting and second-guessing myself. He even made his own copies for backup in case I can't control myself. I'm just spooked about being published. It's bad enough to expose my personal life to speculation, but I'm even more fearful of exposing my shortcomings as a poet. I mean, is Evan really the one to say? I kind of challenged him on his literary expertise.

"Who else would you have judge them, Wynne? Philip? Time to get over that."

Then he asked me how I was doing with this—my

"answer to Nancy"—and if I would actually send the pages back to her, because at some point I just started scribbling on the back of the manuscript. He's seen me doing it.

I said, "I'm nearly out of pages. When I'm done, I'm thinking wood stove."

"Seriously?" he asked seriously. Then he took the hint and threw some more stuff in there.

"I can't even show it to you, Evan, how could I show it to the world?"

"You think she would actually publish it?"

"Showing it to anyone would amount to the same thing."

"I bet there are people who need to read it. Not to snoop into your life, but to dig a little into their own."

(Suspiciously.) "Why do you say that?"

"I don't know everything you've been through. But I'm pretty sure your experiences are not unique. If you have found the words to tell it, you should."

We left it there. Another word from him would set me off accusing him of reading my stuff. But it's me he reads. He says he can see the panicky look in my face when I'm flashing back to "the betrayal"—that's how he sums up everything to do with Bart.

Evan is kind, but kind of dense. No woman wants to read this. No straight woman, and certainly no gay or trans woman. And what could male readers possibly want with it? Only to use it against me, I'm sure. Put me in my place as an artist right quick, they would. I doubt that even Nancy wants to read this, though I thank her for putting me through the exercise. In fact, I think I'll dash off a quick note to her. I still have a few Thank You cards left from one of my weddings. ("Got your package. Thanks for reaching out. Come visit sometime. The caveman wants to meet you.")

We'll see. I have reached the bottom of the back of the last page and there's no more room to practice pithy comebacks.

The question is, how to make the best out of "Making the Worst of Things"?

I'm still thinking wood stove. It's cold in here.

~ ~ ~

Women of the Morning

Women of the morning, look away
Was I talking to myself?
Women of the morning, look away
I'll not be one of you
You who are holding yourselves together admirably
While I am not
And care not if I do

You think you know what I'm going through
But you don't, you don't know me
Women of the morning, look away
I'm not you
And besides, I'm not the clubby type
And besides, it's not like anyone doesn't know how to
mourn
And besides, we have nothing in common, nothing

Then: Good morning!
Two lithe gals jog by, pony-tails swaying
They are fit and perfect and smiling and
So. Young.
Wave. Wave back.
After we have followed them with our eyes
We exchange rueful smiles.

She of Names

I reigned as Queen of the Round Table
Before I stole away and wended widely
Only to be reined in by a Square
Then widow's raiment, despair
Next the aim of a man with an angle
Betrayed, besieged
Then freed
I came full circle
With a champion to claim me
He is made of paint and mists
I am made of tears
Now they call me
Queen of the Rain

Falling Is Easy

Before the apple fell
The apple was offered
Before gravity
Hell

A force applied a pull
Both foot and soul
Secured to soil
Sinking
Naturally

Who didn't notice?
In what time out of time
Were we awareless
Of the downward?
In Eden?
Was the Garden afloat?

Falling is easy
As every creature knows
It is so with or without Newton
With or without God

Take my breasts
When let out of the bra
Take the slick wetness
That tickles inside outside
Singing

Follow me   Follow me down
The fire awaits
And when the fire dies
The cold earth will catch you
There are no high notes to finish this song
We are falling   Only falling

~ ~ ~

Worldwind Books — Powered by Mind

The Worldwind Books Poetry Series celebrates the power of poetry to reveal and to heal with collected works from diverse contemporary poets.

But Who's Counting?
by Zelda Leah Gatuskin
ISBN 978-0-938513-41-4
Funny, poignant, provocative.
NM Book Award Winner

Another Spring
by Robin Matthews
ISBN 978-0-938513-50-6
An evocative portrait of the 1960s and 70s, traced in a spare yet lyrical style.

My Soul's Journey
by W.C. Aldridge
ISBN 978-0-938513-71-1
Broaching truths more often left unsaid, from deep cultural anguish to ecstatic spiritual grace.

www.ingramcontent.com/pod-product-compliance
Lightning Source LLC
Chambersburg PA
CBHW071105260626

47162CB00006B/2212